Eddie

For my grandchildren,
Lucy and Charlie Tame

Published in Great Britain in 2012 by Red Cap Publishing
30 West Quay, Abingdon OX14 5TL
www.redcappublishing.com

Text Copyright © Alan Whichello 2012
Cover design & illustrations Copyright © Stuart Roper 2012

The right of Alan Whichello to be identified as the author of
this work has been asserted by him in accordance with the
Copyright, Designs and Patents Act 1988.

A CIP catalogue record for this book is available from the British Library.

ISBN 978-0-9573411-1-1

The Hamsters' Great Escape

The story of a hamster family's incredible journey

told by

Alan Whichello

Illustrated by Stuart Roper

This is a story about two golden hamsters, Henry and Hattie, who started life in a pet shop in a large Oxfordshire town called Didcot.

Mr Thomas, the owner of the pet shop, was a kind man who looked after them well until they were old enough to be sold.

There were lots of other animals for sale in the shop: rabbits, guinea pigs and gerbils, as well as birds, fish and snakes.   One morning a lady came in with her children, Alfred and Emily. They were twins and it was their fifth birthday.

"You can have any small animal you like," their mother said as the children looked excitedly around the pet shop. Emily walked past Hattie's cage and immediately fell in love with the little golden hamster.

"Can I have that one?" Emily said pointing to Hattie. So Mr Thomas put little Hattie and her cage on the counter.

"What do you want, Alfred?" said his mother

"Can I have that big snake?" asked Alfred pointing to a large snake curled around a branch.

His mother looked horrified. "No, Alfred!" she said. "They are very difficult to keep and they need a large cage. Can't you choose something sensible like your sister?"

"But I like that snake," protested Alfred. Mr Thomas heard what the little boy had said and suggested that he buy another hamster.

"We have just this one left" he said, holding Henry up in his cage. "You can have him at half price, and you could keep him in with Hattie, your sister's hamster."

So Alfred was persuaded to have the other hamster. He quite liked the furry little animal and thought he was very cuddly.

When the family arrived home the children gave the hamsters some food and water.

"Now, you make sure the hamsters have plenty to eat and drink every day" said their mother, "and you must take it in turns to clean out the cage every week."

The children both nodded and began playing with their new pets. Everything went well for a month, the hamster cage was cleaned and they had enough to eat. But the children were becoming bored with the hamsters, and they were playing with them less and less.

There was great excitement in the family's house. Their father had come home and announced "Next week I am taking you all to Disneyland in Florida for 2 weeks holiday."

"But what about Henry and Hattie?" asked Emily.

"Don't worry, one of our friends will come over every morning to feed the cat and she can see to the hamsters as well, so they will be fine," said their father.

The week went by very quickly, the family had packed their suitcases and on Saturday morning their taxi arrived to take them to the airport. Soon the house was empty and Henry and Hattie were all alone.

"I have something to tell you" said Hattie as they both curled up for the night. "I am expecting a baby."

"That's great news" said Henry "when is it due?"

"Any day now" said Hattie. In fact Hattie gave birth to a little boy and girl the very next day.

"What shall we call them?" said Henry.

"I am going to call my little girl Hannah" said Hattie, "you can choose your son's name."

Henry thought for a moment. "I know," he said "I am going to call him Harry." After deciding on the children's names, they settled down for the night.

The next day Henry noticed their food bowl was nearly empty and the water bottle was very low.

"What are we going to do if nobody comes to feed and water us?" asked Hattie. "We have two extra mouths to feed now."

But nobody came to feed them, and the next day their food ran out.

"We will have to break out of this cage and find some food and water," said Henry. "If we jam the food bowl under our running wheel so it will not turn, I can climb up on the outside and see if I can push the cage door open."

The four hamsters pulled the empty food bowl under the running wheel and Henry climbed to the top. He pushed with all his might and the cage door suddenly snapped open. They all climbed up the wheel and out on to the top of the cage. Henry knew they were in the children's bedroom and so he would have to lead his family downstairs to try and find some food.

The cage was on a table next to the children's beds. They quickly climbed down the side of the cage onto the table and then slid down the table leg onto the floor. The door was not quite closed, so they all managed to get to the top of the stairs.

"We will have to climb down there" said Henry pointing to the steep staircase.

"I can't do that" said Hannah, "I might fall!"

"I will help you," her brother Harry said. "Together we can do it."

So they all set off down the stairs. It was a struggle for Hannah as she was the smallest but, with her big brother helping her, they all made it. At the bottom of the stairs there was a closed door leading to the kitchen.

"We will have to squeeze underneath," said Henry. It was easy for Hannah and Harry, but their parents were quite a bit bigger and it took a lot of pushing and pulling before they finally squeezed through the gap.

Henry looked around the kitchen and spotted a large lump of cheese on

a piece of board right by a hole in the skirting board. He immediately went over to the cheese and, with his family following, was just about to take a bite when a squeaky voice said "Don't move!"

Out of the hole popped a big, brown mouse. "What are you doing stealing my food?" he asked.

"Please sir," said Henry. "My family are very hungry, can we have a bite?"
The mouse felt very sorry for Henry and his family. "Very well" he said, "but first I must spring this mousetrap, or else you will be squashed. Now stand back."

The mouse pulled a pencil from his hideout behind the skirting and put it across the trap. There was a loud snap as the spring was released.

"Now you can have a bite" he said to Henry and they all tucked into the cheese.

"Can we have a drink of water?" enquired Henry

"There is a bowl of water over in the corner," the mouse pointed to the bowl, "but watch out for the cat. You would make a nice meal for him."

"Where are you all going?" asked the mouse.

"We are going home to the pet shop where we will be well looked after," said Henry "but first we have to find a way out of the house."

"That's easy," said the mouse, "go across the kitchen floor, through the utility room and past the cat's basket to the gas boiler in the corner. There is an air vent at the side of the boiler  which you should all be able to squeeze through."

Henry thanked the mouse for all his help, then set off across the floor. They were soon in the utility room and could see the air vent at the side of the boiler. But Henry also spotted a large black cat curled up in her basket fast asleep.

"If we go one at a time and are very quiet, then we should make it" said Henry. "Harry, you go first."

Harry tiptoed across the floor and made it to the air vent. Next it was Hannah's turn and then Hattie. Last of all was Henry.

He had crept half way across the floor when the boiler switched itself on with a loud whoosh. The cat opened its eyes and immediately spotted Henry. It leapt up with lightning speed.

"Quick, run!" cried Hattie as she and the children squeezed through the air vent. Henry ran as fast as he could and dived through the vent, just as the cat pounced. He picked himself up and there was all his family waiting for him in the garden.

"Come on" he said "We have a long journey ahead of us."

And they all set off for the pet shop.

They made good progress across the lawn and out onto a footpath at the back of the house. Henry led the way along the footpath until they came to a duck pond

"Quack," said a large white duck who was sitting at the side of the pond. "What are you doing here?"

"Please sir, could you tell us the way to the pet shop?" asked Henry.

"There's only one pet shop in the area and it's down that way." The white duck pointed his wing down the road. "Thank you, Mr Duck" said Henry and the family set off down the road. It was getting dark and Hannah was complaining she was hungry.

"We will have to find somewhere to sleep for the night" said Henry "then we can search for some food."

Suddenly they all heard a strange rustling sound under their feet and out popped a big, black, velvety mole right in front of them.

"What are you doing out at night?" said the mole. "Don't you know there are owls flying around out here that would eat you? Come with me."

He led them down his underground tunnel to the large shelter he had built. "You can stay here for the night" he said. The mole gave them some food and water then settled down in his little nest. The next morning Henry was up bright and early and thanked the mole for his hospitality.

"Could you show us the way to the pet shop please?" asked Henry, but the mole was busy digging another tunnel and was soon out of sight. So they carried on in the same direction.

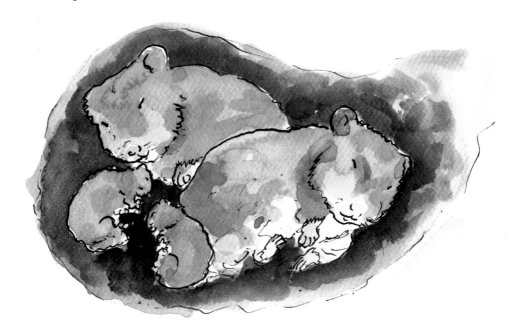

They had come to the edge of the village when they heard a hissing sound.

"Quick, hide in here!" said Henry pulling his children into an empty old bean can.

"Come on out" said a strange hissing voice. "I know you are in there!"

Henry led the way out and there coiled around a tree trunk was the largest grass snake he had ever seen.

"Ah, you will make a nice meal" said the grass snake and began to slither towards them.

"Please don't eat us!" said Hattie hugging her two children. "We have to make our way back to the pet shop." Hattie told the grass snake all about their adventures and all the animals that had helped them.

"Please will you help us too?" she pleaded. The grass snake felt very sorry for the hamster family and said he would show them the way to Wittenham Clumps, from where they might be able to see the pet shop. After following the grass snake all evening they reached the top of the hill.

"I must go back now" said the grass snake. "You will be able to see where you are in the morning." Before Henry could thank him he was gone, slithering through the grass.

Henry found an old rabbit hole and went in to investigate. He came out moments later.

"It's safe down there, there's nobody in" he said, "we will stay here for the night." They had not been asleep for long when a thump, thump, thump woke them all up. They heard something coming down the rabbit hole. A big, brown rabbit with long ears appeared before them.

"What are you doing in my house?" the rabbit said rather angrily.

"Please Mister Rabbit" said Hannah, "We didn't want to get eaten by the owls, so we hid down here." The rabbit soon calmed down when Henry told him their story and how they wanted to get back to the pet shop. "OK" said the rabbit, "you can stay down here, but only till the morning."

"Have you got anything to eat or drink?" said Harry "I am hungry." The rabbit gave them a carrot, some nuts and a drink of water. Then they all settled down for the night, and fell fast asleep. The next morning the rabbit woke them up.

"Come on sleepy heads" he said, kicking Hattie and Henry. "You can show me where you want to go from the top of the hill." They went outside, and Henry climbed up on an old tree stump so he could get a better view.

"We came from over there" said Henry pointing to a little village down in the valley. "And we want to get back over there," he said, pointing to a large town with lots of houses.

"Come on" said the rabbit "I will take you to the edge of the town. From there you must find your own way." The rabbit hopped off in front and Henry and his family followed.

It was slow going in the long grass and the rabbit was soon out of sight.

"Oh dear" said Hattie. "Why didn't Mister Rabbit go a bit slower? Our little legs will never keep up with him, and now we are lost." They kept going all day and finally reached a road.

"If we follow this road" said Henry, "it will lead us into the town."

All of a sudden it seemed
to grow dark, as a big
shadow swooped overhead.

"Quick, run!" cried Hattie
"It's an owl!"

They all ran as fast as they
could into an old pipe at the
side of the road. The owl
landed right by the end of the
pipe and peeked inside, but
the little hamsters were safe.

"We will stay here till the owl goes away"
said Henry. So they settled down for the night,
cold and hungry. The next morning Henry
poked his nose outside. He could not see any
sign of the owl.

"I think it's safe now" said Henry, "let's go
and find some food." They had been travelling
for some time, when they came upon an old barn
on the side of the road. Henry went inside first
and the others followed.

"What are you doing in my barn?" shouted a
big brown rat, who was sitting on a bale of straw
watching them.

"Please, Mister Rat" said Harry "we are all very hungry."

"And thirsty too," added Hannah.

"I suppose I can give you some food and drink" said the rat. "Come with me."
They followed the rat through a tunnel in the straw bales into a big nest that was full of food. There was corn, bread, walnuts, acorns, carrots, potatoes and many more things.

"This is my winter store" said the rat. "Help yourselves." The hamsters had never seen so much food and gorged themselves until they looked like furry tennis balls.

"You had better stay under cover for the night" said the rat. "The barn owl lives here, high up in the roof, and it's not safe for little animals like you."

"Thank you" said Henry. They all made themselves comfortable in the straw bales and were soon fast asleep.

The next morning the rat gave Henry directions and waved goodbye as the tiny family of hamsters set off. They followed the road until it turned away from the town.

"We will take a shortcut across that field," said Henry. "I can see the houses in the distance." They had gone halfway across the field when Henry spotted a deep stream in front of them.

"What are we going to do now?" said Hattie "I can't swim."

"Well, we have to cross the stream somehow" said Henry. "It's the only way."

The little hamsters sat down on the bank.

All of a sudden a big green frog jumped out
of the water and landed right beside them.

"You look very worried" said the frog. "Can I
help you?"

"You could teach us to swim!" said Hattie.
"We have to cross this stream to get to the pet
shop."

The frog croaked with laughter. "I can't teach
you to swim" he said, "but I can
show you a way across.
Follow me."

Henry, Hattie, Hannah and Harry followed the frog along the bank until they came to a tree that had fallen across the stream.

"There you are" said the frog, "you can cross over on the tree." Henry went first, because he was the biggest and heaviest. As he got to the other side he turned and said "Come across in single file, it's quite safe."

Harry went next and made it across to the bank. He was closely followed by Hattie, who also made it safely to the bank.

Then it was Hannah's turn, but she was not very steady as it was quite slippery. Suddenly she lost her grip and plummeted into the deep water.

"Help me!" she cried, "I can't swim." The frog jumped into the water with a loud plop and was soon alongside Hannah.

"Quick, get on this!" he said pushing a lily pad underneath her. Hannah climbed on to the lily pad and the frog pushed her to the bank. She climbed up the bank, dripping wet and thanked the frog for rescuing her.

The relieved hamster family continued across the field until they reached the houses.

"We will cut through the back gardens" said Henry. "There are too many people on the paths, we might get trodden on." So they sneaked into the gardens at the back of the houses. They had crossed about six gardens when they came across a large mound, right in the middle of a lawn.

"What's that?" said Harry pointing to the mound and before Henry could stop him Harry had gone over to the mound and poked it.
"Do you mind?" said a voice. Harry jumped out of his skin and went running back to his father.
"It's a tortoise" said Henry, "I remember seeing them in the pet shop."
"Will it eat us?" asked Hannah nervously, hiding behind her mother.
"No, of course not" said Henry. "They only eat green stuff like lettuce and cucumber."
"Come on, let's go over and introduce ourselves."

They all went over to the tortoise and Henry tapped on his shell. A head poked out on a long neck from the front of the shell.

"What do you want?" said the tortoise in an angry voice. "I was just having a nap."

"We are very sorry to disturb you, but could you tell me where the pet shop is?" asked Henry.

"It's over there" said the tortoise, poking his scaly neck out even more and pointing with his nose. "But it's too far for you to walk there today. It's getting late and there are lots of cats about at this time. You can stay with me tonight where you will be safe."

So the hamster family followed the tortoise into his shelter and settled down for the night.

They were woken the next morning by a loud snuffling noise.

"What's that?" asked Hannah in a rather frightened voice. Henry got up and went to investigate. A big black nose sniffed him as he came out of the shelter. Henry ran back in and hid behind the tortoise.

"Ha, ha, ha," chuckled the tortoise, "I see you have found my friend, Bruce, the black Labrador. Don't worry, he wouldn't hurt a fly, he's just smelling you. He has never seen a hamster before."

The tortoise led the way out, followed by four rather nervous hamsters. Bruce sniffed them all and then said "What are you doing in my garden?"
"Please, sir. We are trying to get back to the pet shop" said Hattie. "Can you help us?"
Bruce thought for a moment and then said "Yes, I can take you to the pet shop, but today is Monday so the shop will be shut. I will take you tomorrow." And then the dog ran back into the house.

Harry looked around the garden and spotted a small ball. "Come on Hannah, let's go and play!" he cried and they both ran over to the ball. Henry and Hattie watched as their children played, happy they were enjoying themselves. Suddenly, a large grey cat leapt over the fence and made a grab for the two small hamsters. But Bruce hated cats and he was keeping a close eye on his garden. He ran across the lawn and chased the cat up a tree. Harry and Hannah ran back to the shelter and hid behind the tortoise.

"It's perfectly safe now" said Bruce, "but you had better stay inside until I take you back to the pet shop." The tortoise gave Henry and his family some food and water and then they settled down for the night, thankful their journey was nearly ended.

It was 9 o'clock when Bruce came out of the house and barked to wake the hamster family. It was a beautiful sunny day. Henry was the first up and came out of the shelter to meet Bruce.

When all the family were outside, Bruce lay down and said "Climb on to my back and I will give you a ride to the pet shop. It will be quicker than walking."

The hamsters tried to stay on the dog's back as he stood up, but they all slid off and fell to the ground.

"This is no good" said Henry, "there's nothing to hold on to." But then Bruce had an idea. He went and pulled the peg basket off the clothes line and emptied the pegs out onto the lawn.

"Now you can all travel in the peg basket" he said. They climbed in and Bruce lifted the basket up in his mouth. Henry and the others waved goodbye to the tortoise as they set off down the path and through the shopping centre. All the shoppers gasped in amazement at the sight of the hamsters looking out of the basket. They soon arrived at the front door of the pet shop at the far end of the town.

Bruce put the basket down and barked. Mr Thomas came out to see what all the noise was about and spotted the peg basket with four little heads poking out.

"Well, what have we here?" he asked, "A whole family of hamsters. Where on earth did you all come from?" He took them into the shop and found a large, empty cage. He filled the food bowl and the water bottle, and then put the hamsters inside.
At last Henry and his family were safe and would be properly looked after from now on, as Mr Thomas decided to keep them as pets for his own children.